THE SCARY HAIR FAIRY

Written by Hannah Russell

Illustrated by Helen Braid

To Mum and Dad,

for making my childhood magical and asking
every day if 'The Scary Hair Fairy' had visited
when I woke up with curly messy hair each day!

x

Gabby

Enjoy Mr Bean,

N.L. Russell

with love x

A dazzle of dust,
a whizz of a wand,
a sprinkle of spark and a moment of magic...

BOOM

the scary hair fairy appears...

The scary hair fairy only appears at night....
she would only appear when there was very little light...

and the stars were shining not so bright...

The scary hair fairy was different
to any fairy known before...

TA
DA!

TOOTH FAIRY

FAIRY GODMOTHER

SCARY HAIR FAIRY

and some would see it as quite a chore...

You know when she's been...

but she's never been seen...

She flutters over your house...

but she's as quiet as a mouse...

In through the door as she patters across the floor.

She *flutters* her wings as she flies among your things...

PITTER, PATTER, without a clatter...

UP
the
stairs
she
goes...

Under the door she slides across your floor...
into your bedroom she creeps...

onto your pillow she LEAPS!

The scary hair fairy likes to play with your hair...

she's always had a * DESIGNERS @ FLARE

A zap of her wand the magic comes from beyond,
with a flick of her wrist your hair begins to...

TWIST
WITH
THE
MAGIC

...leaving it looking a little bit tragic

As the sun rises, she flies as you begin to open your eyes...

it's a little bit BRIGHT

...but you notice some glitter in the light

As you roll out of bed you wonder if it could be true...

one look in the mirror and you KNEW!

THE END

About the author...

Hannah Russell is an author based in the Yorkshire Dales; her first book was published when she was 17 years old about miniature Shetland pony Little Alf. Little Alf stands at just 28 inches high due to him having dwarfism.

As her writing career grew Hannah wrote other children's and teenage fictional stories and has been awarded for her books internationally and had them translated all around the world, as well as having been a best seller on amazon.

Not just books...

As well as writing her stories she is a strong business woman and has multiple businesses based in the UK, working with home interiors, conservation projects and also working as a business consultant on many occasions for small and developing business.

Hannah is a huge believer in helping others and organisations, she is the proud ambassador for 3 charities 'Helping Rhinos', 'Brooke Action for Working Horses, Donkeys and Mules' and 'Wild Welfare', all charities with a mission to help improve the welfare of animals around the world.

Hannah has been involved in many charity projects and campaigns and has even travelled overseas to help raise awareness for causes.

When Hannah is not working, she loves spending time with all her pets in the Yorkshire Dales, she has horses, dogs, guinea pigs, rabbits and chickens! All rescue animals, who often feature as characters in her stories.

Find out more...

www.hannahrussellauthor.co.uk

f @HannahRussellAuthor

⊙ @HannahRussellAuthor

About the illustrator...

Helen Braid is an illustrator based on the beautiful Northumberland coast, which is a constant source of inspiration for her work. Helen first met Hannah when she was commissioned to produce artwork for the Little Alf series of books. She works from a corner of her seaside home surrounded by pens, watercolours, and cups of cappuccino.

You can find Helen at **www.ellieillustrates.co.uk**

Printed in Great Britain
by Amazon

64429864R00015